DIARY OF A KOREAN ZEN MONK

DIARY OF A KOREAN ZEN MONK

DIARY OF A KOREAN ZEN MONK

•

First Edition   December 10, 2010
Second impression of the first edition   September 2, 2015

•

Produced by   Association Of Korean Buddhist Orders
Written by   Jiheo
Translation   Jong Kweon Yi & Frank Tedesco
Illustrator   Dong Han Kyeon
Published by   Bulkwang Publishing
Design   Nabi

•

© Jiheo 2010

•

ISBN 978-89-7479-588-7 (03810)
PRICE ₩15,000

DIARY OF A KOREAN ZEN MONK

WRITTEN BY
Ven. Jiheo

-

TRANSLATION AND NOTES BY
Jong Kweon Yi & Frank Tedesco

ASSOCIATION OF KOREAN BUDDHIST ORDERS

Introduction

The 1700-year old Korean Buddhist tradition has many diverse practices, handed down over the years. Of these practices, Seon (Zen) meditation practice stands out as the most representative of Korean Buddhism. It has thrived over the years in an unbroken lineage. The Seon tradition began to flourish on a wide scale from the latter Shilla Period (9th century) to the early Goryeo Period (10th century) when the Nine Mountain Seon Gate was established. Thereafter, many great Seon masters practiced and transmitted the Seon lineage throughout the Goryeo and Joseon periods.

The contemplative tradition of meditation (Seon) is the path to enlightenment, and is the main Buddhist practice. It has stood the test of time and can be said to be the most authentic practice method.

Every year, over 3000 monks and nuns continue this meditative tradition in the three-month summer and three-month winter retreats in meditation halls (Seonbang) throughout South Korea. *Diary of a Korean Zen Monk* is a three-month record written by Ven. Jiheo of his experience in the Seon retreat at Sangwonsa Temple on Odae Mountain in 1973. Not only is this a good record in which each episode reveals the feel and view of Seon meditation retreats in the

1970s, but also we can really sense the intense energy of the meditation monks seeking enlightenment. Likewise, we can satisfy our curiosity of what happens behind the doors of the mysterious world of the Seon meditation retreat.

The Association of Korean Buddhist Orders has published this book to share with the world the unique and enduring Korean Seon meditation culture. We expect this book will help expand understanding of Korean Buddhism in the increasingly interdependent global community. We hope the foreign monastics in Korea, world Buddhists, and anyone interested in Korean culture will get to know Korean Buddhism more intimately through "Diary of a Korean Zen Monk."

Although Ven. Jiheo's current whereabouts is unknown, we express our gratitude to him for this precious record. It is our hope this book will be widely read as an introduction to Korean Buddhism. We are also grateful for the good translation by Jong Kweon Yi and Dr. Frank M. Tedesco.

December, 2010

Association of Korean Buddhist Orders

*Note: "Seon" is the Korean word for "Zen."

• Nine Mountain Seon Gate : Nine famous Zen centers during the Shilla and early koryo.

Table of Contents

•

THE WAY TO SANGWONSA TEMPLE

•

OCTOBER 1[1]

•

I headed toward the *seonbang* [2] of Sangwonsa embraced by the forests of Mt. Odae. On the way I stopped for a while at Woljeongsa[3]. It looked sad and desolate since it was nearly burnt to the ground during the war.[4] Wind bells that hung from the nine-story pagoda chimed in the breeze. It was disheartening to think how this holy monument had suffered over more than thirteen hundred years.[5]

A meditating stone bodhisattva figure in half-lotus sat near the pagoda. His eternal smile seemed to welcome the gray-robed Seon monks who had come here.

The temple buildings that were rebuilt after the war came into view. The ceramic roof tiles, which once must have been as strong as iron, were gone and replaced by tin and where once had stood round wooden pillars you could put your arms around, I saw only cheap, wooden stanchions. The gorgeous latticed doors were gone and replaced by doors with simple glass windows. It was disquieting to see what had happened to this magnificent temple yet I felt comforted by the monks' vows to restore it. As they swept the burnt foundation stones from under the debris, I felt like bowing to them in reverence. I stepped more lightly toward Sangwonsa.

It's about thirty li[6] from Woljeongsa to Sangwonsa which is a thousand meters above sea level. I finally reached it after crossing streams on stepping stones and passing several slash-and-burn farmsteads.

The Vinaya Master Jajang Yulsa[7] founded Sangwonsa during the reign of Queen Seondeok of Shilla, approximately thirteen hundred sixty years ago. It's been a *doryang*[8] and an active *seonbang*[9] since then. The *jeokmyeolbogung* in Jungdae[10] has continually attracted venerated monks throughout the years.

Jeokmyeolbogung[11] refers to a Buddhist center that enshrines Shakyamuni Buddha's *sari* or holy relics. There are five *jeokmyeolbogungs* in Korea: Tongdosa in Yangsan, Bopheungsa in Youngwol, Jeongamsa on Mt. Taebaek, Bongjeongam Hermitage on Mt. Sorak, and Jungdae on Mt. Odae.

Similar to Jerusalem for Christians or Mecca for Muslims, these places are regarded as holy pilgrimage sites that all Buddhists, ordained and lay alike, wish to visit as pilgrims. Seon monks have favored practicing at this seonbang lately and eating its traditional dish of rice and potatoes (a custom peculiar to Gangwon Province) because the great Seon Master Venerable Hanam[12] used to reside there. You can sense the loving auras of enlightened beings in every corner of this place. Their spirits remain alive in the moss-covered roof-tiles and worn pillars.

Housed in the bell tower, a huge bronze Shilla bell[13] has served the world with reverberations of dharma for more than ten centuries, and images of heavenly beings on its surface inspire us with the Buddha mind.

The short-lived sun of early winter reached the mountains to the west. When I reported my arrival at the *keunbang*[14] , the *jigaek sunim*[15] (guest attendant monk) kindly guided me to a guest room. The room was warm, and the rice and potatoes I was offered tasted like honey.

I was very hungry. I had walked all the way from Jinbu bus station and was exhausted, actually overwhelmed with fatigue. When I notified the wonju sunim (general manager of the temple) and the ipseung sunim (monastic discipline director) of my intention to stay at the temple, they immediately agreed. I didn't go to the keunbang but relaxed in the guestroom instead.

1   This date is according to the lunar calendar.

2   The *seonbang* (선방, 禪房) refers to the room in a temple where meditation practice takes place. It also means the monastery that can offer seasonal retreats. "Heading to the seonbang" is an idiomatic expression for "going to participate in a Seon retreat."

3   월정사. The largest temple on Mount Odae in Pyeongchang, Gangwon Province. Founded in 643 C.E. by Vinaya Master Jajang. Sangwonsa is about a nine kilometer hike away on an unpaved path up through a fir tree forest.

4   The Korean War 1950-53.

5   Woljeongsa Temple was set on fire several times during the war.

6   A traditional unit of measure generally considered to be a little less than a half kilometer.

7   Jajang (자장율사 慈藏 律士 590~658) A renowned monastic discipline (*vinaya*) master of seventh-century Shilla Kingdom.

8   도량(道場). According to *The Encyclopedia of Buddhism, doryang* means a "place of enlightenment" or a "place of practicing the Buddhist way." It is usually understood to be a Buddhist temple that emphasizes both the training and the practice of monks or nuns. Here, *seon dorygang* is a Buddhist temple that functions as a meditation center. A similar term is *seonwon*(禪院), which means *Seon* center or Zen center.

9   Here, it means a temple with a Seon meditation room.

10   中臺. The literal meaning of Mt. Odae is the "mountain with five terraces." They are Dongdae, Sodae, Namdae, Bukdae, and Jungdae, or, respectively, the Eastern, Western, Southern, Northern, and Central Terraces.

11   In ancient Korean temples, there are Korean and English signs that provide a historical introduction and architectural guide to the locale. The following is from such a sign at the *Jeokmyeolbogung* of the Jungdae of Mt. Odae.
"*Jeokmyeolbogung* of Woljeongsa is one of five Buddhist sanctuaries in Korea that have no Buddhist images enshrined inside. This is because these halls were built to enshrine *sari* (Korean for the Sanskrit term *sarira*- calcified remains of a holy person discovered in the ashes after cremation) of Shakyamuni, the historical Buddha. It is said that a revered monk of the Shilla Era (BC 58-AD 935) named Chajang Yulsa brought some of the Buddha's sari from T'ang China during the reign of Queen Songdok (r. 632-647) and enshrined them in Woljeonga . The present building is three-by-three *kan*. (A *kan* is a traditional measure referring to the space between two columns with a hipped-and-gabled roof.) The eaves are bracketed in a double-wing style, which indicates that the structure was reconstructed late in the Choson period. The building is noteworthy because while most Buddhist buildings have latticed doors, this one has two paneled doors at the center and the front is enclosed with grill windows. Also of special note are the decorative end-tiles

shaped like a dragon's head and perched on the ridges of the blue-tiled roof."

12   Master Hanam (한암 漢岩) 1876-1951. He was ordained at the age of nineteen under Master Keumwol at Jangansa on Mt. Keumkang. He entered Mt. Odae in 1926 and never left Sangwonsa. He served as the first Patriarch of the Jogye Order.

13   National Treasure No. 36. The official name of this bell is "Sangwonsa Dongjong" or the "Bronze Bell of Sangwonsa." Near the bell there are signs in English and Korean that read, "This bell, believed to be the oldest and most elegant of Korea' s extant bells, was cast in the year 725 during the reign of King Songdok (r.702-737) of Shilla (57 BC – AD 935) and brought to Sangwonsa in 1469 during the reign of King Yejong (r.1468-69) during the Chosun Dynasty (1392-1910). It is typical of ancient Korean temple bells. Typical features of Korean bells are the dragon-shaped suspension, the flue pipe that protrudes from the body of the bell to set its tone, and the ornamental nipples below the shoulder of the bell. Of special note are the heavenly maidens. They are mingled with the arabesque designs of the bands around the nipples and around to the top of the bell. The strike points are marked with a lotus petal design. The faces and flapping robes of the apsaras between the striking points reflect the realistic sculpturing of Buddhist works from the early eighth century."

14   Literally, "large room." *Keunbang* here refers to the hall actually used for meditation practice. Besides the kunbang, there is a room called *dwitbang* ("back room"), which is, a kind of all-purpose lounge used for personal storage, rest and relaxation.

15   스님. The honorific title for a Buddhist monastic in Korea. Instead of calling their ordination name, Koreans use this honorific title with their assignment to refer to an individual such as like josil sunim or juji sunim. This book follows this practice, too.

KIMJANG

I officially notified the sangha of my desire to stay at the temple after breakfast. Donning my ceremonial robe I made three formal prostrations toward the main entrance of the Dharma Hall. I introduced myself at the admission ceremony. I told the sangha the names of my teacher, home monastery, where I did my last summer retreat as well as my dharma name. The monks who had already gathered at the keunbang neither welcomed me nor rejected me. They simply accepted me.

The seats were assigned according to seniority. Since I am fully-ordained, I was given a seat among the *bhikshus*[16]. As soon as I was seated, the ipseung sunim suggested that we hold a *gongsa.*[17]

A *gongsa* refers to a type of general sangha meeting administered by the principle of majority rule. Once a decision is made, it must be executed. Any issue, whether important or not, can be taken up in this meeting. Issues ranging from *ulryeok*[18] to dismissing a monk from the seonbang are discussed in this meeting. Monastic life does not discriminate between host and guest, nor between oneself and others, and so everything is done in the name of "we." It is imperative to implement rules strictly, inhibiting self-centered behavior as much as possible. Monastic life may appear communistic but it functions democratically.

The topic of today's gongsa was *ulryeok* (collective work) for *kimjang*[19]. No opposition was raised. Since all the monks were going to spend the entire winter there, they reached a quick and unanimous agreement to finish kimjang as soon as possible. There were twenty-three people at breakfast. The wonju sunim and two strong, young monks left for Gangneung[20] to get the spices. After gathering radishes and cabbages from the field, the rest of the monks got busy with the tasks they were assigned.

The middle-aged monks washed radishes and salted

down the cabbages and the elderly monks sorted dried radish leaves. The younger monks dug holes to bury the earthenware pots full of seasoned radishes and cabbages. Everyone worked hard and from time to time snacked on boiled potatoes and cabbage roots. The day was short and the weather was very cold. It was a typical October day in Sangwonsa.

After finishing my kimjang task, I found the *josil sunim*[21] alone, working hard at the discarded leaf pile. He was picking out still-edible leaves. I went over to help him. He quietly told me a story. "Once there were two monks on their way to a hermitage to visit an enlightened teacher. They were about ten li (4 km) away from their destination and about to cross a stream when they noticed a discarded leaf floating on the current. They immediately grumbled, 'Hmph! What sort of enlightened master is he? How can he keep the Way when he can't even save a vegetable leaf? We've worn out our shoes for nothing.' As they were about to give up and return, they heard a shout, 'Hey, monks! Monks! Can you grab that leaf for me? I've been running after it for ten li.' They turned around and saw an old monk running after it. They seized the leaf and were content to resume their steps toward the old monk's hermitage."

The josil sunim, a quiet man, kept gathering the discarded leaves, "You should not waste food under any circumstances. You do not want to disrespect the time and energy people took to prepare it, especially when it's done for others."

What more could I do than keep sorting leaves with him? When Truth is spoken, there is nothing to do but listen.

16   Sanskrit for fully-ordained male monk; *bigu* in Korean

17   공사 (公事)

18   울력 Collective work.

19   In late fall (October-November) kimchi, the spicy Korean cultural side dish, is prepared in bulk in advance of the coldest months of winter season.

20   A major city in Gangwondo province near Sangwonsa.

21   *Seon* Master. The spiritual leader in the seonbang.

PREPARING FOR WINTER AT A MOUNTAIN TEMPLE

Under the wonju sunim'
s direction, we began to make *meju*[22]. A division of labor
is strictly enforced in our collective lifestyle and the many
tasks – which included washing and boiling beans and then
tying and hanging the hard-pressed bricks from the ceiling –
were completed with our cooperative effort. Since there were
many mouths to feed, we had to make many meju bricks but
we finished the work quickly because we had lots of help.

The huge earthenware pot held a hundred gallons of
soy sauce. It was so deeply black that from certain angles
it looked blue or even white. According to the wonju
sunim, you could never have enough soy sauce. No telling
how many visitors might drop in at any time, so you can't

presume to have enough soy sauce on hand.

If you want to sit the winter retreat, you need to assist in kimjang and in making meju. It's an old temple custom. Monks who arrived too late to join in the work offered apologies and volunteered to gather firewood, giving up their daytime Seon practice sessions. Their hard work impressed the rest of us, and soon everyone was working side-by-side.

Heavy snow around Sangwonsa prevents working outdoors between November and early March, and so the more firewood you can collect before the first snow, the better. We chopped down larger trees for a few days. They thundered in the forest when they fell. We filled the large woodshed with logs by the afternoon of the thirteenth.

22 A brick-shaped lump of mashed beans, meju is an important ingredient for all varieties of Korean soy and chili sauces. October by the lunar calendar is meju-making season. As meju greatly determines the tastes of these sauces, meju-making is a much anticipated event in Korean households.

04

GYEOLJE: THE FIRST DAY OF THE RETREAT

It's the day before *gyeolje*[23].
Gyeolje is the first day of a retreat season. A retreat is an all-out effort by Seon monks to achieve Enlightenment. Entering or leaving the seonbang is prohibited at this time.

The annual retreat cycle is set by the lunar calendar. The summer retreat season is from mid-April to mid-July. The winter retreat season is from mid-October to mid-January. Seon monks often call summer and winter "*gongbucheol,*[24]" or the study seasons, and spring and autumn "*sancheol,*[25]" or the free seasons. During the free seasons, monks are free to travel. They prepare for gyeolje during this time.

Monastic life resembles the military in a way. As a soldier prepares for battle, a Seon monk readies himself for gyeolje.

GYEOLJE: THE FIRST DAY OF THE RETREAT

Although room and board is free, the participants are responsible for their own clothing and personal items. I only had some clothes and toiletries and a few Buddhist books. I just had to mend my underwear and socks. I'd be ready after I shaved my head and bathed.

The afternoon was windy, and snow began to fall at sunset. I was happy to see the year's first snow. Several more monks arrived. Others were already sitting inside in meditation, preparing themselves mentally for the arduous months ahead. The wind outside blew snowflakes here and there.

23   결제 (結制)

24   공부철

25   산철

05

RETREAT ASSIGNMENTS

Thirty-six monks participated in the winter retreat. A general meeting was held after breakfast. The *gyeoljebang*[26], the list of seonbang assignments, follows.

|

Josil (組室) or *Seon* Master – spiritual leader of the retreat and *Seon* transmission

Yuna (維那) – Precept Director and leader of posal (repentance ceremonies).

Byeongbeop (秉法) – Monk responsible for temple ceremonies

Ipsung (立繩) – Monastic Discipline Director

Juji (住持) – Chief Administrative Monk, the Abbot.

Wonju (院主) – Monk responsible for practical temple management. General Manager

Jijeon (知殿) – Three monks responsible for offerings to the Buddha

Jigaek (知客) – Monk assigned to hosting guests

Sija (侍者) – Two attendants to assist *Seon* Master and Abbot, respectively

Dagak (茶角) – Two monks responsible for tea service

Myeongdeung (明燈) – lamp lighter.

Jongdu (鐘頭) – Bell ringer

Heonsik (獻食) – Monk assigned to offer food to hungry ghosts

Wondu (園頭) – Two monks responsible for the vegetable garden

Hwadae (火臺) – Two monks responsible for heating the rooms

Sudu (水頭) – Two monks responsible responsible for drinking water

Yokdu (浴頭) – Two monks responsible for bathing water

Ganbyeong (看病) – Monk responsible for nursing the infirm

Byeoljwa (別座) – Kitchen Master

Seoki (書記) – Monk responsible for paper work

Gongsa (供司) – Two monks responsible for the staple foods

Chaedu (菜頭) – Two monks responsible for preparing side dishes

Bumok (負木) – Four monks assigned to collect firewood

Soji (掃地) – Monk responsible for general cleanup

I'm a *bumok*. I'm neither satisfied nor dissatisfied with my work. I simply accepted it because communal life requires me to discipline myself. After the service to celebrate gyeolje, the josil sunim gave the following Dharma talk.

"Nothing is permanent, everything is eternal. As for the form of things, we see impermanence, but in their Original Nature, we see the eternal. On the one hand, we deny the eternal because humans are mortal, but we affirm the eternal because of our human potential. The suffering and attachments of sentient beings negate eternal life, but thanks to Buddha's attainment of nirvana, we can have faith in the eternal. Let's put aside our human limitation and develop our potential to the utmost. Like animals in winter stroking their pregnant bellies dreaming about the joy of future offspring, like seeds about to sprout in the frozen ground, let's cultivate our Buddha nature this winter in order to attain Enlightenment by coming spring. Buddha nature is in ourselves and eternal."

Both the monk giving the talk and those who listened deeply resolved to achieve Enlightenment that winter. Some gritted their teeth and others clenched their fists in determination.

Tea followed the formal Dharma talk. The ipseung sunim posted the timetable.

2: 30 a.m.	Wake Up Call
3:00 a.m. – 6: 00 a.m.	Seon Practice
6:00 a.m. – 8:00 a.m.	Cleaning, breakfast, rest
8:00 a.m. – 11: 00 a.m.	Seon practice
11:00 a.m. – 1:00 p.m.	Lunch, rest
1:00 p.m. – 4:00 a.m.	Seon practice
4:00 p.m. – 6:00 p.m.	Dinner, rest
6:00 p.m. – 9:00 p.m.	Seon practice
9:00 p.m.	Sleep

Repentance ceremonies would take place in the morning on the last day of every month.

At one in the afternoon the slap of the *jukbi*[27] resonated in the keunbang to mark the first Seon session. Every monk sat facing the wall in the lotus position. The room was silent; you could barely detect the sound of breathing. Everyone was intent on Enlightenment. No one moved. They were all wall-gazing Buddhas. But what about their minds?

Seon monks can be compared to soldiers in battle. As a soldier is judged by his actions on the battlefield, a Seon monk is recognized for wisdom cultivated in the seonbang.

26   결제방 結制榜 It is also called *Yongsangbang* (龍象榜). This system of assigning jobs originated in *The Pure Rules of Pai Chang* (白丈淸規), written in T'ang Dynasty China. Assignments can vary from one seonbang to another according to the need of each temple. The list of assigned jobs is usually posted in the seonbang during the retreat.

27   죽비 or bamboo clapper. In Seon practice, jukbi is used to announce the beginning and end of the practice session. It is also used to alert practitioners who are drowsy or daydreaming during meditation sessions.

THE ECOLOGY OF THE SEONBANG

The members of this seonbang were very diverse. Their ages ranged from sixteen to seventy comprising three generations. They represented all eight Korean provinces and often reminisced about their hometowns. You could guess their whereabouts by their accents. Most of those from the northern provinces were middle-aged or older.

Some had no formal education but others had graduate degrees. As for formal Buddhist education, one had not even taken the minimal *Admonition for Beginners*[28] course at Sutra School,[29] but others were sutra masters who had completed the Great Teaching Course.[30]

Some monks were from upper-class families and some

were poor. This shouldn't be a problem in a seonbang but the penchant for "birds of a feather flock together" was obvious during breaks. This probably couldn't be helped since we're still unenlightened beings. Such a mixed membership might lead to conflict in the secular world but it wasn't a problem for us.

Although we were living together communally, our focus was on our personal spiritual achievement. You must take the first step to the last by yourself in order to attain Enlightenment. The means and purpose derive from inner resolve, too. Any talk of the "big I" is inauthentic without having already attained Enlightenment.

It may seem uncaring to lead such a self-centered life. This is understandable because the slightest deviation can bring a Seon monk's pursuit of the Way to an end, and he simply becomes a lazy freeloader. The way to Enlightenment opens only with adamant resolution. No matter how much I think about this, I always reach the same conclusion: The pursuit of Enlightenment begins with the "I" in chaos and ends with the "I" in harmony, from the "I" in turbulence to the "I" in tranquility. Restless when he begins on the path, the Seon monk struggles to escape that anxiety forever. The spiritual journey is risking everything to gain true life – this is the ecology of monks in a seonbang.

To be altruistic, you should be extremely egoistic. Isn't it paradoxical?

28   초발심자경문(初發心自警文) or Chobalshimjakyeongmun. This book instructs novices in the manner and practice of monastic life. A classic of Korean Buddhism, novice monks and nuns are required to study this book at the Sutra School.

29   강원(講院) or a "gangwon" is a sutra school, one of the three fundamental institutions in a traditional Buddhist monastery, together with 선원 (禪院, *seonwon* in Korean) or the Seon center and 율원(律院, *yulwon* in Korean) or the vinaya school.
A sutra school is divided into four levels: 沙彌科 ("*samigwa*"), 沙集科 ("*sajipgwa*"), 四敎科 ("*sagyogwa*") and 大敎科 ("*daegyogwa*"). It takes five or six years to complete the entire course.

30   대교과 大敎科

A SEON MONK'S KARMA

Three rules of seonbang life have been handed down over many generations: Keep your mind fresh, your feet warm, and your stomach partially empty – eat no more than eighty percent full. These are succinct guidelines that characterize the simple life of Seon monks.

There are no blankets in the seonbang. When sleeping, seonbang monks cover their feet with the same cushion they meditate on. As the cushion serves a dual purpose, Seon monks always carry one in their *barang*[31] when traveling.

A Seon monk eats about three *hops*[32] of grain a day. For breakfast porridge, for lunch steamed rice and for dinner rice with mixed grains. Side dishes are mainly vegetables, and once in a while, bean cake and brown seaweed are served as special dishes.

The following is the annual physical consumption of a typical Seon monk.

Food: 3 hops of rice x 365 days = 51.3 Gallons

1,095 *hops x* 15 *won*[33] = 16,425 *won*

(Each monk must provide whatever other food he wants.)

Clothing: 20 yards of cotton cloth x 50 *won* = 1,000 *won*

Underwear: 1,500 *won*

Shoes: Two pairs of rubber shoes x 120 *won* = 240 *won*[34]

All in all Seon monks can live on twenty thousand *won*[35] a year. It's an unwritten rule of Seon monks to accept as their fate the Three Lacks – lack of food, clothing, and sleep.

The pursuit of desire leads to unpleasant results. Although Seon monks aren't totally free from desire, they try to keep distant from it. Lay people respect this vow. This is why even seventy-something lay Buddhists are sometimes the first to bow to those grey-robed monks who are their junior.[36] When you spend time around them, though, you can't help but notice that Seon monks become embarrassed and fearful just like ordinary people. In fact, they are completely ensnared by desire but their passion is one that worldly people rarely even dream about: They are enticed by the great desire to become a buddha who transcends life and death. They wander through steep mountains and deep valleys, committing themselves to austere ascetic practices like the wall-gazing Bodhidharma. To aspire to "no desire" is also a great desire!

Seon monks recognize that human beings are creatures of suffering. They know that they are yoked to suffering: They are clothed in suffering, dine on suffering, and dwell in the home of suffering, surrounded by a wall of suffering. The only thing Seon monks can rely on is the will to overcome suffering. They are aware that if they fail to maintain this focus, their lives will end in catastrophe. Accordingly, they have no choice but to hold on tightly to this goal.

A Seon monk is not a product of fate but a creation of karma. Fate is what was determined for you before you were born, and there's no way you can change it; karma refers to what you choose with your own free will in the present. Thus, fate is inexorable but karma is malleable; fate is fixed while karma can be changed by your intentional actions; fate implies limitation and karma confers possibility.

It was my fate to be born poor but it is my karma (actions) to become rich when I grow up. It is my fate to be born a human and not a louse or a flea but it is my karma to choose Buddhism as my spiritual refuge and aspire to Enlightenment.

"I" exist as the object of my fate and the subject of my karma. My fate was determined in the past when I was not there. But karma is something that I can control myself in the present. Accordingly, I can always create and reshape my karma until the last moment of my life.

Once the inevitability of fate is understood, you also realize the rationality of karma. Fate is never something to bemoan but something to accept, just as karma is something to embrace and love. If a Seon monk is able to love his ragged robes, the symbol of his own elected suffering, he is on the threshold of Enlightenment, holding the door knocker in his hand. As the Seon monk becomes used to his disciplined life, he senses more strongly that karma is something he should uphold wholeheartedly.

31   바랑 Traditional monk's cloth sack.

32   홉 A traditional unit of measure about 0.18 liter.

33   Korean currency is called won.

34   These are 1970s prices. Rice now costs about 150 *won* per *hop*. Buddhist clothing shops in Seoul sell cotton cloth for 10,000 *won* per yard. The plain thin rubber shoes, popular among monastics, range from 3,000 to 4,000 *won*.

35   In 1972 when this diary was written, the exchange rate of was five hundred *won* per U.S. dollar. That makes twenty thousand *won* equivalent to about forty dollars.

36   The etiquette of the Korean custom of honorific bowing is determined strictly by age: The younger bow to their elders first. The author indicates that practice differs around monastics because of the respect due them.

POSAL: REPENTANCE CEREMONY

It's the last day of the month. It's also the day for shaving our heads, bathing and doing laundry. We have to wear long underwear in the winter to stay warm. It's difficult to avoid killing lice who've made home there when we scrub them.

It's scary to see a sharp blade skimming across my scalp but it's cool and refreshing to have my head shaved smooth. What a difference between seeing and feeling!

The junior monks offered the small bathroom and laundry room to the senior monks for the winter retreat. They walked down to the brook instead where they broke the surface ice to wash their clothes and only bathe themselves where they must because it was freezing.

Posal[37] or repentance ceremony was led by the *yuna sunim* in the afternoon. The *Vinaya Pitaka* from the *Tripitaka*[38] was recited, and the Ten Precepts for novices[39] and the 250 Precepts for bhikshus were explained.

Seon, in principle, is teaching outside of the sutras. It proclaims "Directly point to the mind and attain Buddhahood" or "Attain Enlightenment without depending on words or letters," emphasizing the importance of seeing your Original Nature. Seon monks exclusively focus on their hwadus. They reject any unnecessary rituals or other religious practices. They even dispense with the sutras. As a consequence, Seon monks often look strange and obsessed. Although the yuna sunim sensed that it would be pointless to discourse on precepts and bodhisattva action to such monks, he did so anyway, and the sangha simply listened.

Some monks didn't pay the slightest attention and just concentrated on their hwadus. Others left at the beginning of the ceremony and walked around outside. No one objected to this ritual. Everyone seemed to accept that everything in the world had a purpose, necessity, and historical nexus. As long as you're not enlightened, you don't know what's right or wrong or what's real or phony. In other words, an extremely conservative 'wait and see' attitude pervades the tradition. Is it because of the *Jebeop jongbonnae*[40]? Or because things exist for the sake of existence itself as existentialism asserts?

In the world of sentient beings, if you emphasize practicality too much, it's a way of justifying anything, and if you emphasize a principle too much you create dogma. Therefore, Seon monks who desire to escape the world of sentient beings through Enlightenment simply try to see and feel the world as it is like witnesses. As long as you're in the world of sentient beings, all judgment is up to the mind of sentient beings. Accordingly, the Buddhist family considers it taboo to judge what's right and what's wrong. But, in fact, they never stop judging because they're sentient beings, too.

37 Sino-Korean transcription of the Sanskrit word, *poṣhadha*. "The bi-monthly ceremony held alternately on full-moon and new-moon days. It is required of monks and nuns according to the rules of the Vinaya. The central practice is a recitation of the monastic rules as contained in the *Pratimokṣa-sūtra*, followed by

public confession of any transgressions of them. According to the rules of the *Vinaya*, it should be performed by all the monks of a particular area and should occur within an established boundary and according to a prescribed formula⋯" From John Powers, *A Concise Enclopedia of Buddhism* (Oxford: Oneworld, 2000). P. 163-164.

38   The Three Baskets. The Buddhist canon consisting of the Vinaya, Sutra and Abhidharma pitakas or baskets.

39   Kwan Um School of Zen translated the ten precepts as follows: "1. I vow to abstain from taking life. 2. I vow to abstain from taking things not given. 3. I vow to abstain from misconduct done in lust. 4. I vow to abstain from lying. 5. I vow to abstain from intoxicants, taken to induce heedlessness. 6. I vow to abstain from going up on a high podium, and all prideful show. 7. I vow to abstain from using adornments, perfumes, and ointments. 8. I vow to abstain from all amusements such as shows and dancing. 9. I vow to abstain from handling gold, silver, money, and gems. 10. I vow to abstain from eating at unseasonable times, and from keeping pets." From *Dharma Mirror: Manual of Practice Forms*, complied by Merrie Fraser. p. A.22.

40   A phrase from the *Lotus Sutra*. *Jebeop jongbonnae* is the first part of the couplet that reads "諸法從本來 常自寂滅相." Burton Watson's translation of this line is: "All phenomena from the very first have of themselves constantly borne the marks of tranquil extinction." From *The Lotus Sutra*, Burton Watson. New York, Columbia University Press, 1993. p. 37.

THE SEONBANG'S AMBIENCE

The history of a seonbang is made in the *dwitbang*.[41] Let's look at what happens there.

The dwitbang is a long rectangular room immediately beside the *keunbang*. It functions as a multi-purpose rest area for the seonbang. The monks' barangs that hold their personal belongings and toiletries are stored there side by side on shelves, so the room is open to everyone. During breaks, the monks congregate in small groups and exchange informal dharma talk or chat. Others rest on their backs or practice yoga in order to relieve muscles cramped by sitting in lotus for long periods. The room also functions as a dispensary where ill monks are treated and convalesce. Some monks sew torn garments or read sutras. Others compose letters or scrawl in their diaries.

Just as a seonbang has a recognized josil sunim or Seon Master, there is another 'teacher' in the dwitbang. While the josil sunim in the keunbang is chosen by the sangha because of his wisdom and knowledge of the dharma, the *dwitbang josil* or dwitbang master is chosen because of his ailments and gift of gab. While formal history of a seonbang is made in the keunbang, it is in the dwitbang that its informal history is made.

The hierarchy of a dwitbang is often decided by how much time is spent there. Monks who spend a lot of time in the dwitbang sit less in the keunbang and gradually lose standing as Seon monks.

The position of Sangwonsa's dwitbang master went to a *hwadae sunim*, a monk in charge of the rooms' heating. It was a unanimous decision by the sangha since he's had ulcers for ten years and served as dwitbang master in renowned monasteries such as Haeinsa and Beomeosa.

The dwitbang master had advanced education before he entered the mountains, and completed the Four Great Teachings when he became a monk. He spent more than a decade residing in temples, and sat in major seonbangs across the country. Accordingly, he was regarded as best qualified to be dwitbang master by the entire sangha. He's talkative, melodramatic and a showman. He has a charming accent from the Gyeongsangdo region where he was born and grew up. Even should the Nakdong River[42] dry up, this dwitbang master's never at a loss for words! He can be paradoxical and pitiful, too, at times. He even seems enlightened occasionally because of what he says and does, but he acts like a devil sometimes, too. He curses and praises Buddhas and patriarchs and arbitrarily denounces universally respected masters, even putting them down as hopeless dullard.

Despite his pretentious, know-it-all attitude, the sangha doesn't shun him because he's basically a good man, a kind of comedian, and is fun to be around. Though he's not respected at all, he's a perfect dwitbang master.

There are times when he loses face and his position's challenged. The wonju sunim's the reason. The wonju sunim frequently goes to Gangneung to purchase commodities because he's responsible for managing temple operations. He stays at the propagation center in the city and gathers news about temples around the country. Since transportation's speedy nowadays, he can pick up scoops faster than the newspapers.

The wonju sunim is also a good talker. Whenever he returns with scuttlebutt gathered during a trip away, everyone in the dwitbang wants to hear. Our frowning dwitbang master, ignored and disregarded by the sangha, is compelled to listen like everyone else. At each pause in the wonju sunim's talk, he quickly cuts in with a joke or cynical comment to get everyone's attention. When the wonju sunim's through, the dwitbang master seizes the stage, calling attention to himself with peculiar gestures. He's anxious to regain the spotlight. Acting like a silly buffoon, he keeps jabbering ceaselessly while the rest of us, long accustomed to his antics, pay him no heed.

41　　　뒷방 dwitbang means "back room".

42　　　One of the longest rivers in Korea which is in the Gyeongsando region.

MATERIALISM VS. SPIRITUALITY

Can Enlightenment be achieved only by self-mortification? I think about this a lot. There are a few monks who practice in extreme ways in our seonbang. Seon monks are often thought of as "eccentric practitioners" but that title should be given only to the few monks practicing in extreme ways.

There was a controversy concerning whether to admit a monk who eats only raw food to the winter retreat. After a long and heated discussion, the sangha decided to accept him on the condition that he should eat alone in the dwitbang. He was given an easy assignment – *myeongdeung* or lamp lighter.

One of the *sudu* sunims who is responsible for

drinking water eats only one meal a day[43], and a *wondu* sunim who works in the garden doesn't eat in the afternoon[44]. The *ganbyeong* sunim or nursing monk, practices never-lying-down-to-sleep[45], and a *yokdu* sunim, who is in charge of bathing water, keeps strict silence[46]. The only sound from his mouth is an occasional cough, and he communicates only through writing.

Whenever I encounter monks who go to extremes by restricting their already humble diet or by torturing their limbs that have already been strained from sitting twelve hours a day or by vowing silence, I feel pity for them rather than respect. Unsurprisingly, they argue that they have good reasons for these practices. They claim they want to eradicate karmic obstacles which are heavier than others, or they don't deserve three meals a day because they haven't accumulated enough merit.

One day an interesting discussion took place in the dwitbang. "What's more important, the body or the mind?" the *jijeon* sunim (ritual director) asked. He had studied science before he ordained and he scoffed at the "eccentric practitioners" in the seonbang.

"There's no question about this. The mind is more important. What a silly question for a Seon monk to ask! If you have nothing better to say, you had better chant," a *bumok* sunim (wood gatherer) with a liberal arts education retorted sarcastically.

Most Seon monks denigrate rituals like offering ceremonies. The bumok sunim was a hard Seon practitioner and had been uncomfortable with the jijeon sunim's presumption of expertise on Buddhist ritual. He had been telling us that monks should be well versed in rituals if they want earn their own living.

"What do you think sustains the mind?" asked the jijeon sunim. The jijeon sunim and the bumok sunim started to argue stridently.

"Of course, it's the body."

"Yeah! Just like a tree without roots cannot produce leaves, the sky without clouds cannot produce rain. Likewise, how can the mind exist without a body? Remember that the mind appears only after the body comes into existence.

"Please, stick to logic and common sense! We're not talking about hwadus that are beyond logic but talking about the nature of the mind and body using reason. This issue is really turning into a debate about materialism versus spirituality. That being said, your support of materialism is ridiculous. Don't forget that we're in a seonbang, a center of spirituality. It's commonly recognized that the body is mortal while the mind is eternal. Just consider the sublime character of the mind as compared to the fragility of our bodies that are doomed to decay as we grow old."

"Don't talk abstractions or quibble about words! Let's just focus on practicality. It's a biological fact that a sound body makes for a sound mind. There's no doubt that the body precedes the mind. To expect a sound mind in a sick body is like hoping for fresh growth from a dead trunk."

"Look! Look at all the successful examples of abstinence that speed up spiritual progress. I don't have to illustrate this point because they're happening all the time. Although I won't even attempt some practices because I'm not good enough, just look at those monks who renounce comforts to pursue Enlightenment. Look at those who eat only once a day, who don't eat after mid-day, who never lie down to sleep and who practice silence. What great challenges to our contemptible body by our sublime minds! ”

“Practicing like this is artificial, hypocritical and just a way to show off. Genuine seekers should take care of themselves. You can attain *lianzhi*[47] through well-being, and Enlightenment comes only after lianzhi.”

“Don’t be deluded by the *Wu-wei*[48] of Laozi and Zhuangzi. They simply turned away from the world, and only cared for ease. They could not reach their goal of Sagehood[49], so they didn’t even try to save the world and relieve people of suffering. We strive for the ultimate goal of Enlightenment, disregarding our bodies that will inevitably pass away. Enlightenment is necessary in order to save sentient beings.”

“Don’t forget that we’re only sentient beings caught in an endless cycle of rebirth with all our karmic burdens. Do you honestly expect to liberate yourself when you aren’t well?”

“Absolutely. That’s why we’re here on this mountain, enduring a life that’s nearly hell.”

“Stop misleading suffering beings with words like that! You’re claiming that Enlightenment is only possible when you cripple yourself! The Buddhist vinaya stipulates that the physically disabled cannot ordain. This rule reinforces my argument that a sound mind requires a sound body. A healthy and balanced constitution is essential for Seon monks like us on the path to Enlightenment, Nirvana, Perfect Virtue and Tranquility."

"You choose to remain a prisoner of your fickle body while it's comfortable and healthy at any cost, and you gaze at sentient beings with heavy karmic debts as if you were a lifeless Buddha statue."

"Lest I should become such a lifeless Buddha statue, I take care of my body. Why have I chosen to endure this difficult seonbang life? I want to feel the suffering of beings with oppressive karmic debts! Now, let's stop this talk. I care for my passing body, not because I cling to it as you think I do. Actually, I'm not attached to it at all. Your body is not just something you observe, but something you should feel. Look at it this way. We've left the world not because we don't love it but rather because we love it very much. We love the world so much that we have to keep a distance from it in order to see it and feel it more honestly. We struggle for Enlightenment away from the world so that we can eventually make it whole. We're very far from the world, and it's very imperfect and it's going to remain as it is. If the world fell completely apart, there'd be nothing we could do about it then, even if we were enlightened. Do you understand what I'm saying? Let's stop here. It's time to sit."

The argument ended without conclusion.

It's hard to judge what's right and what's wrong in the world of sentient beings. It's because sentient beings are dualistic beings made of both right and wrong.

43   일종식(一種食)

44   오후불식(吾後不食)

45   장좌불와(長坐不臥)

46   묵언(默言)

47   양지(良知) *liangzhi* ("good conscience") A Taoist term meaning innate knowledge or a primordial existential awareness possessed by every human being.

48   무위(無爲) An important concept of Taoism meaning 'effortless action' or 'taking natural action.'

49   지인(至人) In the Taoist tradition, the Sage refers to the person who gained wisdom that extends beyond mere intellectual knowledge or information and reflects a deep, intuitive understanding of life.

INSTINCT AND SEON MONKS

The eleventh lunar month is severely cold at Sangwonsa. Dawn breaks late here since the temple is surrounded by mountains. The watery, white porridge we ate for breakfast tasted like honey since our stomachs were empty. We ate dinner around five p.m. yesterday and it was completely digested by midnight.

Kimchi in Sangwonsa is so salty that some say that it's saltier than salt produced in salt flats in Ju An[50]. To abate their hunger, junior monks eat it as if it were salad. Fortunately they don't have to worry about dehydrating because the stream in the Sangwonsa valley never dries up, even in winter.

For Seon monks, next to the hwadu, the most insistent

thought is about food. The craving for food strongly suggests that monks haven't really eliminated their desires, but that they have merely deflected them or put them on hold. It also demonstrates that the most basic human instinct is to consume food. I've concluded that the most compelling human fear derives from hunger.

Just as concentrating on hwadu can lead to Enlightenment, concentrating on food can lead to a General Sangha Meeting. It was decided to offer a special meal to the sangha the first and fifteenth day of every month regardless of the difficult economic straits of the temple. The special meal consisted of glutinous rice and dumpling soup.

The authority of the General Sangha Meeting is more powerful than martial law. Once a decision is made, it must be carried out. Even if it agreed to butcher a cow, it has to be implemented no matter what. If the General Sangha Meeting decided to sell the temple, then it must be done. The entire sangha takes responsibility for the decision. The meeting is run very democratically and, in most cases, it reaches reasonable conclusions after thoughtful consideration.

Although the salty taste of kimchi at Sangwonsa

exemplified the frugal way the wonju sunim managed temple finances, he was obliged to release glutinous rice, red beans and laver that he had kept in storage.

As the aroma of the red beans boiling in the kitchen wafted through the keunbang, the sound of swallowing was heard from the sitting monks in both rows as they began to salivate. Distracted by their sharply developed olfactory sense as good as hunting dogs, the hungry monks dropped their hwadus and began to daydream about the delicious dinner. In their mind's eye, each savored a steaming seaweed-wrapped bundle of glutinous rice in his mouth and after chewing delightedly, let the rice morsels slip down his gullet into his belly that suddenly extends from his spine. Catching themselves, they straighten their backs and return to their hwadu with greater resolve. How poignant! How innocent! How pitiful! A bowl of glutinous rice is a great energizer for practice.

Thoughts of revenge and desire for victory appear more spiteful and cruel inside oneself than outside. Everyone could eat as much as they wished. The monks, who were almost always hungry, took revenge on their hunger by gulping down as much as they could without concern for their stomachs.

The specialty vegetables of Sangwonsa were served on top of the glutinous rice, and they made the special meal even more special. All the monks emptied bowls that had been full to the brim, and exclaimed that they were as happy as the governor of Pyongyang[51], slapping their bellies. I commiserated with the raw-food monk but he said that he enjoyed the meal, too, because he ate the glutinous rice anyway.

A sutra teaches: "Do not love anyone, do not despise anyone. You suffer because you can't meet the one you love often enough, and you suffer because you encounter those you dislike too often." We should remain distant from the feelings of love and hate. Live with detachment. The monks knew this teaching better than anybody else yet they violated it because of hunger. They overate. Instant karma.

More than ten monks were absent for the afternoon Seon practice session. Three or four monks left the seonbang in the middle of the practice due to acid reflux and excessive saliva. Some of the monks who remained in lotus succumbed to drowsiness and kept nodding off.

Although there are differences among individuals, statistics indicate that about ninety percent of Seon monks suffer from gastrointestinal conditions. That they're pathetically defeated by their instinct to eat is obvious. Old, ailing Seon monks, who haven't attained Enlightenment go from dwitbang to some old pantry with hands on their stomach under the scornful glare of junior Seon monks. Eventually they'll die with no one to care for them. The life of a Seon monk is a double gamble – a gamble against secular life, and a gamble against monastic life.

There's usually not enough food but there were leftovers this time after dinner. The monks who were still belching with indigestion didn't show up for dinner. Some monks who disliked skipping meals sat for dinner anyway, and spooned rice into water and gulped it down quickly as if they were eating porridge, something they'd never normally do. The keunbang was almost empty in the evening Seon session. Only flies filled the room, fluttering freely. The dwitbang was full, though. The dwitbang master beamed with a broad smile on his funny face.

When I stretched out to sleep, the jigaek sunim who

was lying right next to me, wished to talk. He graduated from college and completed the Great Teaching Course at a sutra school. He's a quiet person and doesn't get involved in debates among monks.

"Is suppressing human instinct a virtue or not? What do you think?"

"It can be virtuous to develop spiritual faculties, but it's not good for physical balance. It's bad for young people but it's neither virtue nor vice for older ones. "

After a while, he asked me again.

"Must a Seon monk suppress his instincts to attain Enlightenment?"

"The mere suppression of instinct may not be enough. There're both sufficient conditions and necessary conditions. Suppression is a necessary condition and Enlightenment is the sufficient condition. Necessary conditions are means, and there can be several means. If suppressing instinct is a mean, on the contrary, satisfying instinct can be a mean, too. Without suppressing instinct or a necessary condition, the sufficient condition can be met and you can attain Enlightenment as long as you are true to your own self-nature."

"If the suppression of instinct is the only variable in this function, self-nature may represent the constant. Given this, is it possible that the function works without variables?"

"You can't apply mathematical theory to the theory of Seon. Remember that the former belongs to physical science, and the latter belongs to metaphysics."

"If the suppression of instinct is a necessary condition and True Nature is the sufficient condition, are you saying that Enlightenment is possible without the necessary condition as long as you meet the sufficient condition?"

"Yes. In metaphysics, a possible thing is possible from the beginning, and an impossible thing is impossible from the beginning. Only inevitability matters here, with all sorts of practical limitations and possibilities excluded. I may sound like I'm babbling. I don't know which side I am on, possibility or impossibility. I'm just making an effort, hoping that it's possible. The die is already cast."

"What a horrible gamble."

"Yep. It's scary, too."

"This is a proposition that makes me think a lot."

"It's not a proposition. It's a question. You can answer it

when the sufficient condition is satisfied. Let's sleep. Too much thinking kills the mind and too much eating kills the body."

Icy gusts sweep across the earth with a roar.

50   A town near Incheon in Korea famous for producing salt.

51   The governor of Pyongyang symbolizes one of the highest and happiest governmental positions in an old Korean proverb.

OLKKAGI AND NEUTKKAGI:
AGE OF ORDINATION

The josil sunim's *sija* is sixteen, and the Juji's *sija* is nineteen. They're the only monks here under twenty. They're also small for their age so we call them "boy sunims." Both are orphans. The josil sunim's is "little boy sunim," the Juji's is "big boy sunim."

The "little boy sunim" was brought to the temple when he was five by a neighbor who was a lay member of the temple. His late parents worked as day laborers. He's been here for about twelve years. The "big boy sunim" is from Naksan Orphanage that's run by a Buddhist foundation. He moved into the temple after graduating middle school. He's been here about four years.

We have a lot of sympathy for the two boys. To be

made to wear monk's robes so young is both a blessing and a challenge. They usually get along with each other well enough but sometimes they're antagonistic.

When in harmony, they address each other with the honorific title "*sunim*." But when they're upset, they call each other bad names. The younger calls the older "*neutkkagi* [52]," and the older fires back, "*olkkagi.*[53]"

It's generally acknowledged that human sexual desire emerges around the age of ten. The Buddhist clerics who are ordained as young kids are referred to as "virginal ordainees" or "olkkagi." Olkkagis tend to look down on neutkkagis, claiming more entitlement in the monastic life in the name of their "virginal ordination."

At Sangwonsa, if the age criterion to distinguish olkkagi and neutkkagi is fifteen, thirty percent of the sangha is olkkagi and seventy percent neutkkagi. If the criterion is twenty, seventy percent are olkkagi while thirty percent are neutkkagi. We estimate that the majority of monks ordain around age twenty.

Naïve about temple life at first, a neutkkagi is like a docile, newborn calf. He absolutely obeys the olkkagi. But as he becomes accustomed to temple routine, the neutkkagi surmises that olkkagis are no different than they are except that the olkkagi has spent more time mooching temple food without attaining Enlightenment, no different than any other worldly being. Consequently, a neutkkagi can rebuke an olkkagi as "temple rice thief." Though sounding rude, these pejoratives are also goads to practice harder: Make the most of your precious time!

An olkkagi grows up both physically and spiritually in a temple so they are unpolluted by corrupt worldly life and a bit awkward about mundane things. Immersed in temple culture, they are well versed in rituals and put great importance on precepts. They're brought to the temple as small children, and didn't choose to live this hard life. They're likely to become attached to the external things of religious life and get hung up on style and mannerisms.

In contrast, a neutkkagi has chosen to enter the monastery. Some cynical critics say that only losers or dropouts who don't have the courage to commit suicide escape to mountains to become monks. This may be partly true. Okay. Even if you were a loser before ordaining, once you enter a temple and begin monastic life, everything changes. The monastic life forbids the five desires[54] and seven emotions[55], and you'll have to bear with the three lacks.[56] You'll soon realize that the way to Enlightenment is long and hard, and there're many days that you'll have to live in adverse circumstances before you "enter into nirvana."[57] If you joined the sangha because of some naïve idea about monastic life, you will soon experience worse frustrations than you suffered in worldly life. The question arises. Stick it out or return? Most people return to the world. Those who choose to remain make a decisive commitment with all their being for the rest of their lives. We call this decisive commitment a "vow."

People in the outside world are often surprised to learn that someone "left for mountains" to become a monk. Why did such a capable fellow flee to the mountains? What a waste! People gossip. They are right in a way. A person like this never hesitates; he simply plunges into temple life and dares to live on sad 'monastic offerings'. As precious sons and daughters in their families outside the monastery, they have to put up with the humiliating label "neutkkagi" in the monastic life.

They don't express complaints, dissatisfaction or irritation. They think that since their karma brought them to the mountains, they have to be grateful for being admitted into the sangha. They made their vow when they recognized their causal conditions. They already know that temple life does not guarantee nirvana or Enlightenment but a painful and difficult life. They willingly accept frustrations and are confident that they will eventually attain Enlightenment.

The Buddhist family puts stress on vows and causal conditions. The *Beopseonggye* or *Gatha of Dharma Nature*[58] declares "Arousing the mind to the Way is Enlightenment itself," and the Buddha himself said "I cannot save sentient beings who don't have the right causal conditions." It is essential to vow and create right causal conditions in order to live as a monastic practitioner.

You should renew your vow over and over, and strengthen your causal conditions whenever you can. Being sons and daughters of Buddha, they should hold their vow and causal conditions tight in both hands.

By writing this, I don't imply that only neutkkagi have such a vow and causal conditions. To avoid this misunderstanding and criticism from olkkagi monks, I, a neutkkagi monk, think I need to state some facts concerning olkkagi monks.

From an olkkagi's viewpoint, the world isn't a sea of suffering. The tourists and visitors who visit the temple look just as nice and happy as can be.[59] Although they learned from senior monks or sutras that the world is the vast ocean of suffering where sentient beings live with heavy karma, they had never felt it themselves.

When we say we yearn for nirvana, paradise, transcendence, tranquility, and strive to attain Enlightenment, it means that we really want to experience these spiritual attainments personally.

As for educational institutions for monastic members, there are some Sutra Schools installed in a few major temples of the Jogye Order[60]. However, those schools teach only canonical studies. So some monastics make their ways into urban areas after their Sutra School in order to learn other things besides Buddhist texts. While Dongguk University, founded by Jogye Order, Masan College and Wonkwang University offer broader programs, these schools were not only founded for monks but mainly for regular college students with interests in Buddhism. What frequently happens in these circumstances is that approximately nine out of ten monks attending these schools become secularized. They are outnumbered by regular college students and their faith gets weakened by what they experience on campus.

School expenses for olkkagi monks who study in the city are also a problem. Only a few monks receive full financial support from their *Eunsa*[61] or home temple and are accepted to live in a dormitory or a branch temple. Most have to earn their expenses through part-time work in private temples in the cities.

There are olkkaggi monks who mainly concentrate on pure practice in the mountain temples, too. They are not distracted by non-canonical studies or urban life. The Ministry of National Defense does not leave them alone, however. Without exception, every male Korean citizen who reaches the age of twenty receives a letter of conscription. Once you receive the letter, it is mandatory to change from gray robe to military uniform. And, once you are in the army, inevitably, you will be treated like an ugly duckling – either in a good sense and bad sense. After three years of memories and experiences of army life, where bawdy talk is everyday language, how many olkkagi monks do you think return to temple life with a pristine beginner's mind?

As for the olkkagi monks who left for secular education in college and other institutions, how many of them, too, do you think return to temple life with a shining beginner's mind?

How many olkkagi monks return to a mountain Seon center after completing courses at Sutra School? There's one answer to all these questions: Extremely few.

***

The boy monks got into a fight this afternoon. A dust cloth triggered the fracas.

The younger boy monk has a responsible attitude and is quite orderly. He's very independent, straightforward, neat and self-effacing – common characteristics among olkkagi monks.

The older boy, however, is shrewd and slippery. He's a survivor, "gets by," quickly calculates his gains and losses, and follows a labor-saving 'middle path,' cutting corners when performing duties assigned to him. Although it's been four years since he was brought to the sangha, he still has the mindset of a kid from an orphanage.

The younger monk had a dust cloth he reserved exclusively for cleaning the josil sunim's room. He always kept it clean and tidy and stored it in a special place. He always washed it right after using it. In contrast, the older boy monk doesn't have a dedicated dust cloth for the juji sunim's room. He usually cleans the room when the juji sunim is out. He uses dust cloths from other rooms, and never returns them to places where he found them. It's a practice he hasn't changed in spite of several warnings.

The bigger boy was severely scolded by the ipseung sunim because of the dust cloth today. He didn't return the younger sija's dust cloth after he took it without permission. The older boy believed that the younger snitched on him and got him in trouble.

After the ipseung sunim's scolding, the older boy went and stared down the younger monk. A storm was looming. The "low barometric pressure" brought on by the hostile stare affected the weather between them. It brought dark clouds and accompanying lightning and thunder.

The seonbang monks were chatting and relaxing in the dwitbang soothing their strained legs after a difficult sitting session. The older sija was lying on his back waiting for an opportunity to take revenge. Just at that moment, the younger boy inadvertently stepped on the elder's foot while he was lowering his back sack from the shelf. For the elder sija, it was a lucky chance, but for the younger, it was only a minor accident. The two began quarreling, swearing and shouting derogatorily "neutkkagi" and "olkkagi"at one another. They pinched and kicked and struggled and the older punched the younger in the nose. The younger reacted impulsively and head-butted him back with all his might. Blood shot from both the 'big nose' and the 'small nose' spattering red splotches on their robes and the floor. The scuffle was immediately stopped, and the youngsters were brought to the ipsung sunim. After being sternly reprimanded on their knees before him, they were dispatched to the Buddha Hall to prostrate a hundred and eight times to repent their folly.

After the bell sounded to announce lights out, I heard the two sijas jabbering happily on their sleeping mats by the altar. They're as unpredictable as summer storms; even before the sun had set, they were friends again and seemed inseparable.

52   늦깍이] A slang or derogatory title for a monk who ordained in his/her old age. Its literal meaning is "late shaver" or someone who tonsured when quite mature.

53   올깍이] Slang for someone tonsured at the proper age. Here that age is assumed to be around ten or before puberty.

54   The desires for wealth, sex, food, fame and sleep.

55   Pleasure, anger, sorrow, joy, love, hate and desire.

56   Lack of food, clothing and sleep.

57   A Buddhist idiomatic expression meaning "die." The phrase is usually used when a Buddhist monk or nun dies.

58   법성게 (法性偈) or *Gatha of Dharma Nature* composed by Master Uisang (CE. 625 - 702)

59   Many traditional temples are located in the National Park areas of Korea and are visited by all variety of tourists, not just temple members and dharma practitioners. Many temples are designated secular National Cultural Properties by the Korean government and are treated accordingly.

60   조계종 The largest Buddhist organization in Korea. It comprises about 2500 temples and more than 10,000 monastics. Most traditional temples in Korea, including Sangwonsa and Woljeongsa, belong to the Jogye Order.

61   은사(恩師) meaning 'graceful teacher.' An aspiring monastic requires a seior monk who accepts, trains and supports a new candidate. An eunsa sunim is like a father. An eunsa and his disciples function as a form of family unit in monastic society and their relationship is usually life-long.

13

A TREACHEROUS APPETITE

Baked potatoes at Sangwonsa are simply awesome. Maybe the ravenousness of the poor monks who live here has something to do with it. They're mouth-watering. Even rich city folk who visit the temple can't resist them.

Here's what happened a few days ago. When the blaze in the fire hole of the *ondol*[62] underfloor heating system cooled down, a stealthy monk buried an armful of potatoes stolen from storeroom under the glowing embers. Between the last Seon period and lights out, the monk on secret "baked potato duty" went to the fire hole to fetch them. His accomplices, awaiting the purloined potatoes, licked their lips in the dwitbang.

The potatoes were thoroughly cooked after a few hours in the embers. A delicious aroma arose from the burned potato skins when peeled back. The potatoes tasted like roast chestnuts. Eating three or four of them surely drove the hunger pangs away. The monks got charcoal black around their lips while peeling the burned potato skins open. They had to grin when they espied one another. They were both titillated and rewarded by the secret potato rendez-vous!

At first, the "potato party" of a few monks led by a hwadae sunim assigned to heating ondol rooms met in front of the fire hole. The party later moved to the dwitbang. They could gather there because the wonju sunim slept in another building far from the keunbang.

As the number of partiers swelled, more potatoes were consumed. The monks rotated clean-up duty to thoroughly dispose of any evidence of potato after the secret feasts. Meanwhile, the wonju sunim, who was very conscientious about inventory, noticed a sizable loss of potatoes every night. He didn't directly interdict the party by raising the issue at the General Sangha Meeting, however. He installed a hasp and locked the storeroom door with an old padlock instead. Still, the potato feasts continued. Among the party members was a monk who could defeat any kind of lock only with a nail and a nail clipper. The wonju sunim didn't foresee that such talent existed in the sangha.

The wonju sunim returned from Gangneung after some research to stanch the 'outflow' of potatoes. He immediately hung a new, heavy-duty padlock with a secret code number on the storeroom door.

Nonetheless, the feasts didn't stop then either. One day it was a *wondu* (gardener) sunim's turn to bake potatoes. The forty-something monk had a unique habit. No matter what temple he visited, he would bust off the hinges of any locked door he encountered. He believed that Buddha's disciples shouldn't have anything to hide or valuble enough to steal. He said he felt frustrated whenever he encountered a locked door. It reminded him of the sad bondage of sentient beings who are entrapped by ignorance and rotten karma.

Well, the gardener monk succeeded in removing the hinge of the storeroom door that the wonju sunim had locked so confidently. The wonju sunim got very serious while the potato lovers couldn't hide their smug grins.

The wonju sunim's not the kind of person who would give up easily and simply leave the storeroom to the potato thieves. After a few days of reflection, he came up with a strategy, and quickly put it into action. He decided that potatoes would be the main dish at Sangwonsa.

The ratio of rice to potatoes, which had been six to four at the mid-day meal, became four to six, and fifty-fifty for the evening meal became three to seven. Potato soup and fried potatoes were served at every meal, too. Facing collective complaints from the sangha about the glut of potatoes, the wonju sunim declared:

"You guys eat potatoes every night even sacrificing your precious sleep. I learned quickly how much you love potatoes. I'm serving you plenty of potato dishes just to satisfy your craving. I promise you I'll change the menu in a week."

The sangha grew tired of spuds very quickly. The potato feasts came to an end and potato devotees didn't gather in the evenings anymore.

The wonju sunim won the game, knowing full

well how fickle human taste buds are. What a tactic! We recognized that our wonju sunim was one of the best wonjus in the entire Jogye Order, no doubt about it.

62   *Ondol* is a traditional heating system in Korea. Ondol system heats the floor of the room, channeling heat through flues from the fire hole in the kitchen. The heat generated by the fire can be used for both cooking and heating at the same time.

HWADU

A month has passed, and differences in practice have begun to appear among the monks. Seon monks live with their hwadu. Hwadu means "true speech" by which a Seon monk intensifies meditative concentration.[63]

A hwadu is given by the josil sunim when a Seon monk is admitted to the retreat for the first time. There are innumerable kinds of hwadu, but out of the many hwadus, a serious practitioner needs only one. A hwadu works best when a practitioner uses only one exclusively.

The hwadu that most Seon monks employ is *Shi-Sam-Ma*[64]. From of old, monks from the Gyeongsangdo region have been the majority in Korean monastic society and though we are far north in Gangwondo, the Gyeongsangdo dialect still prevails. As a consequence *Shi-Sam-Ma* is *I-mo-ggo*[65] here.

Hwadu is a religious faith, not a philosophical proposition. That is why it is practiced on the basis of faith, not analysis.

Hwadu is a means, not a goal, toward Enlightenment. Any means can be justified when the goal is attained, and any hwadu can be justified as long as it leads to Enlightenment. Any discourse concerned with good and bad qualities of a hwadu is delusion. A good Seon monk does not pull hwadu, he is pulled by hwadu.[66]

A novice at Seon practice, especially if he happens to be intellectual, tends to be analytical about his hwadu. Enlightenment can only be attained through the contemplation of absolute nothingness that is severed from the relation of being and non-being. If a Seon monk tries to understand this principle of Seon intellectually, the more he tries, the more his effort will be in vain. He will be totally stuck in his own mind and body.

However, as you spend years sitting in seonbangs, you will realize that, unknown to yourself, your intellectualism and tendency to analyze will have been replaced with an empty mind and the hwadu. Finally you will have become a Seon monk in a true sense. Every temple posts the following admonition above its entrance door.

Ip Cha Mun Nae Mak Jon Ji Hae

入此門內 幕存知解

This phrase means that any knowledge gained outside this gate is useless inside of it. A hwadu turns a Seon monk either into an idiot or a genius. The idiot is released from pain because of his idiotic qualities. The genius suffers because of his genius. Great stupidity leads to great wisdom, and great suffering leads to great liberation.

The practice of a Seon monk can be judged depending on whether he pulls his hwadu or he is pulled by his hwadu. A Seon monk pulled by his hwadu is calm. A Seon monk pulling his hwadu is unstable.

Half of our sangha at Sangwonsa practice well while the rest have trouble. The monks sitting in the upper row are calm while the monks in lower row are unstable. Seats are assigned according to the order of receiving the Bhikshu Precepts. The monks in the upper row sit like mountains. Monks in the lower row appear as restless as summer weather.

The monks in the lower row clear their throats, make dry coughs, switch legs in the lotus position to soothe their pain, straighten their backs, shake side to side and back and forth, blink eyes and change the positions of their hands. All this happens because they try to pull their hwadu rather being pulled by their hwadu. For these monks, the jukbi announcing break time will surely sound like "Hallelujah!" So long as they endure the initial pain and remain in the seonbang, the time will come when they'll be able to enjoy the Seon sessions so much that the jukbi is simply a sound.

Every monk experiences these phases of seonbang life without exception. It's because Seon is the essence of Buddhism as well as a shortcut to Enlightenment. Some monks avoid seonbang life because they can't overcome the discomforts of the early stage.

There is a monk in our sangha who suffers from severe neuralgia. This monk is pulled by his hwadu. He sits one hour and does two hours of walking meditation in the temple out of every three-hour sitting session because of his pain.

He does walking meditation in the early morning and late evening without fail in his rugged monastic robe despite the snow and cold wind. He keeps regular practice time just like other monks. What commitment! It would be impossible if he wasn't pulled by his hwadu.

63   *Hwadu* is literally translated as 'head of speech". Jogye Order of Korean Buddhism, Seoul, 2004.

64   시삼마 (是甚麼) Chinese character meaning "What is this?"

65   이뭣고 *I-mo-ggo* means 'what is this?' in Gyeongsangdo dialect.

66   What the author means by "pull" and "be pulled" is a key point to understand the relationship between a Seon practitioner and his hwadu. Here, "pull" and "be pulled" are literal translations of Jiheo's personal expression about his hwadu practice. If a Seon practitioner tries to understand or solve or master the hwadu, he calls it "pulling" the hwadu. Here, the practitioner and hwadu exist as two separate entities. This means that the practitioner did not enter a state of no-self, which is the essential condition for Enlightenment. On the other hand, if a practitioner is "pulled by" the hwadu, the author implies that the practitioner "becomes as one" with his hwadu. This means the practitioner attained the state of no-self in his pursuit of Enlightenment through his hwadu.

A SICK MONK

A monk who suffered severely from tuberculosis prepared his back sack to leave today. Although he wasn't well enough to practice, he practiced hard anyway. He began coughing up blood yesterday. He had to leave. Tuberculosis is epidemic now, and the seonbang is a public place.

He tried very hard to smile even when he was coughing blood. This was admirable. He was a forty-something monk who entered a monastery as a child. He had no place to support him. Although he said that he didn't know where to go, he didn't appear discouraged or concerned. He just showed quiet acceptance.

A fundraising effort was suggested by the dwitbang josil. Despite the dire circumstances of Seon monks, every sangha member dug into their pockets and bags and offered the little they had. The sick monk had impressed them very much. We raised a total of 9,850 won. The temple office offered 5,000 won, and two monks donated their wrist watches. Fortunately, I had extra underwear. I put it in his back sack.

Tuberculosis requires long-term care. He didn't have enough money to enter a hospital or a tuberculosis sanatorium, only enough for first-aid treatment.

He put on his back sack, thanking us for our generosity. He said he was very sorry to distract the sangha from practice, and begged forgiveness. Coughing, he left along the narrow mountain trail in the snow. The trail was like the course of time. It's a way of no return, and probably a path to the other world.

Where does life come from? Where does life go? I felt very sad. There's no guarantee that I won't be in the same situation as the sick monk. I'm discouraged. It may be natural for me to feel like this since I haven't attained Enlightenment.

In modern Buddhist circles, monastery residents who become ill have nowhere to go. What is more, a Seon monk, for whom the hwadu is everything, has no place to rely on. There are more drugstores, and bigger hospitals nowadays – all of them profess medicine for everyone, but they're not generous enough to help Seon monks who have nothing but their hwadu. Although they may call themselves "the Family of Compassion," Buddhist temples aren't kind enough to extend shelter for a sick Seon monk. All he can expect is a backroom of a nameless hermitage if he is lucky. He'll be comfortable there when he dies.

A good Seon monk should preserve his health well. He should be very careful because Enlightenment is not achieved quickly and diseases are jealous of Enlightenment.

A healthy *Seon* monk resembles Buddha, but a sick monk is uglier than a married monk. Being sick, he wanders around in search of medicine in a mean and abject manner. Having forsaken his hwadu, he is no longer a Seon monk, but somebody we call "human trash."

Nothing is more important than your body. Next to the hwadu, this truth should be kept in mind by a Seon monk. He should not dismiss it as being too worldly and materialistic just because he is pursuing a noble, spiritual life.

16

YONGMAENG JEONGJIN: INTENSIVE PRACTICE

December has come. When the winter retreat enters the second half, every seonbang observes Yongmaeng Jeongjin practice. Yongmaeng Jeongjin refers to the practice of never-lying-down-to-sleep. This practice continues an entire week.

It's 9 p.m. The sleep demon began to attack me. It's the first crisis of the first day. Despite the continuous warning sound of the jukbi, my eyelids keep closing as my head tilts forward. The sound of the jukbi was like a lullaby.

After thirty minutes of blinking eyes in fatigue, my drowsiness left and I went out to wash my face with cold water. I was refreshed. Tea and snacks were served at midnight, and we had few minutes' break. Relaxing our legs with walking meditation, we sat again. What a long night! Alas, morning came.

A day passed, and two monks dropped out for physical reasons. Two days passed, and three gave up. The third day came. It was the last crisis as well as the most difficult period of Yongmaeng Jeongjin. Every joint was aching in the evening of this day. I felt pain even in my hair and toenails. The sleep demon attacked me in every pore in my body. My hwadu slipped away like a sly fox. My tongue tasted as bitter as gall, and my stomach ached terribly. My mind became numb. If I could lie down with my arms and legs stretched wide, then I'd have been freed from this pain immediately. If I did, though, all my efforts in this Yongmaeng Jeongjin would have been wasted.

I tried to visualize the extreme ascetic practice of holy teachers.

"Six years in the snowy mountains."[67]

I managed to open my eyes and straighten my back. My eyelids dropped again and my back bent forward.

"The cross of Golgotha."

I was able to open my eyes again and straighten my back. But, shortly afterwards, my eyes closed again, and my back bent forward.

Half asleep and half awake, I heard the snores of a monk snoozing in the dwitbang. My drowsiness and pain suddenly disappeared. My hwadu encouraged me to speed up. It urged me on, saying, "It may be a long and hard but hang in there, you'll make it."

The Buddha taught: "There is nirvana, and the path to nirvana, and the Tathagata[68] who teaches the way. Some people are able to attain nirvana and others cannot. The Tathagata can't do it for you. I can only show you the way."

Buddhism emphasizes the human role in causes and conditions.

Sometimes it appears that liberation comes unexpectedly. Out of innumerable situations in everyday life, one event can suddenly bring you Enlightenment. Buddha attained Enlightenment when he saw the morning star. Rain water in a human skull precipitated Master Wonhyo's[69] Enlightenment. Master Seosan[70] became enlightened on hearing a cock crow early in the morning.

Causal conditions that may bring about liberation do not come like a miracle. When you don't surrender at the peak of suffering but embrace it, you will finally meet the right causal conditions and attain Enlightenment. The most extreme pain inevitably leads to peace. Because death comes only once, it is not a challenge for someone who has overcome it.

I was able to defeat the sleep demon thanks to the snores in the dwitbang. I usually fall asleep myself when I hear someone snoring but not this time.

Five more monks dropped out on the third day. All the monks who endured the first three days successfully completed the intensive practice.

It's Buddha's Enlightenment Day December 8th according to the lunar calendar. We finished the Yongmaeng Jeongjin early in the morning.

We were offered steamed sweet rice for breakfast. The entire sangha ate well. We then climbed to Jungdae to pay homage to the Buddha at the Jeokmyeolbogung, and returned by way of Bukdae. Hiking the snowy mountain trail was difficult, but it was great fun.

67   Korean temple paintings depict Buddha's six-year long pre-Enlightenment ascetic period as sitting in snowy mountains.

68   Tathagata is the name the Buddha when referring to himself.

69   원효 (617-686 C.E.) One of the most revered monks in the history of Korean Buddhism.

70   서산 (1520-1604 C.E.) A patriarch in Chosun Dynasty. His formal Dharma name is Hyujeong.

BROKEN SPIRITS

As December deepens, heavy snows fall often. The world went completely white.

The monks who failed to complete the Yongmaeng Jeongjin became lazier and lazier. They spent more time in the dwitbang than before. Perhaps they were uncomfortable because of their failure. Although the ipseung sunim warned them to keep the on-going practice schedule, they did not follow suit. They only grimaced, saying they were sick.

A warning is given three times. If you don't comply after three warnings, that's it. More than three times is unnecessary. No one can play your part as a monk but yourself.

The monks who successfully completed Yongmaeng Jeongjin became more energized and made more effort in their practice.

Three monks in the dwitbang left with their back sacks. There'll be no more chance to live in a seonbang for them.[71]

They are sicker at heart than in their bodies.

71   Seonbangs have a very strict rule about monks who leave a retreat early. A record remains if a monk did not successfully complete a three-month-long retreat season.He/she will not be allowed to participate in other retreats there and at other seonbangs.

A SPECIAL MEAL

The day for dumpling soup. Under the supervision of the wonju sunim, the entire sangha worked together. While the filling was prepared, monks sat in a circle making dumplings. The filling consisted of bean sprouts, shiitake mushrooms, kimchi and seaweed chopped into small pieces. Some monks kneaded the dough into thin dumpling skin, and cut out round pieces using a kettle lid. Other monks put in the filling. Some dumplings looked pretty, some were crude, and some dumplings split because of too much filling.

There are monks that are always on the lookout for mischief, and whenever an opportunity presents itself, they jump to it whatever the consequences. Some kneaded the dumplings to look like female genitalia, and some shaped them into penises. Funny. The subconscious reveals itself in situations where sexual instinct is suppressed. Maybe that's why religious art is graphic in expressing male and female features.

The joking did not stop here. One monk stealthily filled dumplings with ground red pepper powder. Another put salted sesame seeds in his dumplings. Another filled his with chopped radish. The dumpling soup was finally ready. It was a special meal and I was given a brimming bowlful of it, and I ate as much as I wanted. It was good.

The unfortunate monks who had fallen victims to the "special dumplings" began moaning and shouting. "Ouch, too hot!" a monk who bit into a red pepper dumpling cried out. "Oh, salty!" a monk who ate salt dumpling blurted out.

While some were grimacing or making loud noises, others were giggling at the plight of the victims. One giggler suddenly gasped when chewing into a mischievous dumpling. Of all the sangha members, the ipseung sunim, the sternest member of the seonbang, chanced to get a red pepper dumpling. Blowing hard, and slurping soup in a near-panic, he smacked his lips over and over. No cries or gesticulations, though. What a seonbang veteran he was!

Venerable monks usually eat very quietly in a solemn atmosphere. Once a bite is in your mouth, you have to chew it with your mouth firmly closed so that it can't be seen. You can't spit out food or make any noise before you swallow. This doesn't mean that you shouldn't chew well. Chew enough, but quietly. You can't make any noise with your chopsticks or bowls, either.

The whole process of dining is very hygienic. Everybody has their own personal bowls, and washes them themselves. The spoon and chopsticks are kept in their own cloth pocket. There's a wrapping cloth and a wiping cloth for bowls to whisk away dust, too. The wiping cloth is washed every few days; it has to be clean all the time. There are alms bowls that are inherited over several generations because they are kept so well. They are considered very prestigious.

The meal offering was messy and tumultuous due to the mischievous monks. After the meal, the josil sunim gave a talk with a somber voice.

"This is an old story about a meal time in a monastery. The josil sunim, who was eating at his seat, happened to notice a dead mouse in the bowl of a novice sitting near him. The novice held up his bowl and quickly swallowed it. That very moment, the Buddha on the altar extended his hand, and stroked his head. If the novice had made a scene, what would have happened? You can't make a ruckus and disrupt meal time no matter how unappealing the food might be. Let us repent the karma of those who played with this precious food. They betrayed the spirit of generosity with which it was offered."

The mischievous monks bent their heads in shame, and the victims blushed. The ipseung sunim was embarrassed, too. The special meal became a sort of punishment. But the josil sunim's teaching was a wonderful incentive for our spiritual growth.

NEW YEAR'S EVE

It's the last day of the year. We spent the day working together making rice cake and cleaning up. I washed clothes and took a bath. I couldn't sleep immediately. It may be because it's a very special day.

New Year's eve reminds me that I must review the year just passed. Humans are different from animals not just because they can assume an erect posture but because they have a consciousness that can reflect on the past.

If you spend the year repeating one unvarying day after the next, do you really need to reflect on it very much? In fact, you need to examine it even more carefully. New Year's Eve demands it of me. In retrospect, I made a lot of mistakes.

I didn't make any resolutions at the beginning of the

year. I didn't have the motivation, and I wanted to avoid the frustration of not meeting my goals. I assumed then that I would have nothing to regret about the year, but I did. A great sense of emptiness overwhelmed me.

I started the new year in a hut on Mount Taebaek, working on my hwadu. Although my hwadu practice did not progress at all, my body changed quite a bit since last New Year. I lost a tooth, and I have more wrinkles on my forehead and deeper valleys between them. I have less hair with less color and gloss, too.

At the end of the year when you're obliged to repay your debts, I'm unable to do so. Thanks to the immeasurable mercy of Buddha, I was able to stay at a seonbang. Thanks to the offerings given to me here, I'm able to sustain my body. But I still haven't attained Enlightenment. How can I repay the kindness given me! I shudder in bitter regret.

But it's New Year's Eve. The year's almost over and it's nearly midnight. We're reminded to put the past behind us and have the courage to tear off the last page of the calendar and put up a new one.

Humans can't live in the past. We can put down

yesterday's burdens in order to live for tomorrow. While my hwadu demands that I change quickly, it pulls me into a deep slumber instead.

A mountain dove cried through the night. It sounded like a sorrowful Auld Lang Syne.

THE LONELINESS OF A SEON MONK

It's the first day of the year. Whether they want to or not, Seon monks live apart from their families and hometowns. Their memories are vivid, though, because Seon monks are humans, too. While they are more strong-willed than other people, they can be very sensitive at the same time.

We had a day off from practice today. The dwitbang was crowded. The monks were from different provinces, and they talked about their special regional New Year dishes and costumes. Even at other times of the year, food occupies more than half the conversation of Seon monks. Monks from same province get together. Birds of a feather flock together.

All of us played *Yutnori*[72] in the afternoon, betting on

roast potatoes. Although we all had full stomachs, roast potatoes are always tempting. Sangwonsa potatoes have a distinctive taste that neither gourmets nor gluttons can resist. The Gyeongsangdo party won the game, and we all ate potatoes.

Darkness fell and I felt very empty. I felt the same way yesterday. Was it because it was the last day of the year? Why do I feel this way on New Year's Day? I'm lonely to the bone. My worldly attachment that had been dormant deep within me suddenly arose. Whenever this happens, the only solution is to be more faithful to my hwadu. This is why a Seon monk needs to be alone.

The *Nirvana Sutra* teaches that a practitioner should remain alone to win the battle with himself, which in itself is a difficult enough task.

Li Bai[73] sang about loneliness in his poem *Drinking Alone by Moonlight*. "A cup of wine, under the flowering trees; I drink alone, for no friend is near. Raising my cup I beckon the bright moon, For her, with my shadow, will make three people. The moon, alas, is no drinker of wine; Listless, my shadow creeps about at my side.[74]"

Nietzsche lamented: Whenever my mouth sings, no

one listens but my ears.

This is the starkest loneliness! Yet it is the will of a Seon monk to pursue liberation in his profound loneliness.

My hwadu inches ahead like a turtle while time sprints like a hare. I can't abandon my hwadu for a moment!

Seon monks are blamed for being stubborn, egoistic and self-righteous. I don't take this as criticism; it's true, and it's how Seon monks should be.

There's a Buddhist saying: "Unless you are free from attachment, you can't be liberated from rebirth."

If so, should I (Tathagata) abandon the attachment that only I can save sentient beings? Subhuti asked. "Does the Tathagata desire to be the Tathagata? If he does, he falls into the trap that the idea of self is real. If he does not, how does he save sentient beings?"

A Seon monk without attachment to self is like a Seon monk without a hwadu. As long as you remain a Seon monk and seek Enlightenment, you must strengthen yourself and be faithful to it.

When I stretched out to sleep, the jigaek sunim who was lying beside me whispered.

"We've gotten a year older."

"That's true."

"I fell backwards in my practice last year. I'd be happy if I don't fall back again this year. But I'm not very confident about that."

"It's difficult work. Ordinary people get poorer as they get older, and monks who don't make effort become lazier and more hypocritical the longer they keep eating temple food. If we can't make progress, we should at least try hard to stay where we are."

72   윷놀이. A Korean traditional game with four sticks. Usually all the family members play together on the first day of the year after the new year's memorial service for the ancestors.

73   이백 (李白) A Chinese poet in Tang dynasty (701-762 C.E.)

74   Translation by Arthur Waley

A HYPOCRITE MONK

The monk who's been eating only raw vegetables and uncooked grains declared that he would begin a solitary fasting retreat at the Mountain Spirit Shrine. He looked very weak, and they said that he had eaten only uncooked grain for six months. He was much weaker than the first time I saw him here at Sangwonsa.

He went to the monastery right after high school graduation. He reads too much and his knowledge is unorganized, even excessive. He's an erudite man, but not at all profound. He is extremely introverted and very intent but he's physically weak and quite irritable. Though knowledgeable in diverse subjects, he's arrogant and hypocritical. With less than five years of monastic experience, he pretends to have attained Enlightenment, which is ridiculous in the eyes of senior Seon monks. In short, he is a Seon Pierrot, a kind of unwitting clown. He talks slowly with his legs crossed in lotus position and his eyes slightly closed even when he addresses his seniors. On the other hand, he can suddenly become hysterical if anyone gets on his nerves in the slightest way, and reacts in a tirade and acts out with all kinds of gestures. Does he eat raw food to accelerate his practice or just to show off?

Even the dwitbang master, who hates to lose any kind of encounter, disliked to argue with this monk. The sangha members in general did not like his odd way of acting and speaking, and they finally turned away from him. Completely alienated from everyone, he decided to make another attempt to show off his superiority in the seonbang. Thus the solitary fasting retreat. It was a dangerous thing to do considering his health. It shouldn't be permitted in this freezing cold weather.

I sat in front of him after the mid-day meal. It was my first time to talk with him.

"Sunim, are you going to do a solo fasting retreat? It's

freezing outside and the Mountain Spirit Shrine is very cold···"

"I know. But I can't tolerate everybody freeloading here on donated food in the cozy indoors and always wasting time with useless arguments in total delusion. It's quite pathetic."

How condescending! But I refused to argue with him because we differ in many ways.

"So, you're gonna wipe out karmic debts on behalf of stupid sangha members?"

"That's right. With my fasting prayers."

"That's a very generous of you, sunim. By the way, you said you mastered *Zhuangzi*. Do you remember the episode about walking in Handan?[75] A boy from the Yan state went to Handan, the capital of Zhou Dynasty, to learn how to do the Zhou style of walking. But before he was able to learn it, he forgot his own way of walking, and eventually had to return on his hands and knees."

"Yes, I do."

Step by step I tried to catch him off-guard.

"Then, do you remember the episode of Xi Shi's frowning face[76]? The beautiful lady Xi Shi went around with her face in a frown. An ugly lady thought her pretty, and went around the village emulating her. Rich people shut their doors on her, and poor people left the village with their families."

"I remember it, too," he responded irritably as if he was offended.

"Sunim. An hour of sleeping reclined on your back is better than three hours of sleep in sitting position or five hours of sleep while standing up. If you ignore self-nature and do unnatural things, you will inexorably fall into delusion. Neglecting your well-being for the sake of asceticism may be meaningful for religious observance, but it won't enhance your spiritual practice a bit. I think it's better to practice asceticism for self-help rather than self-abuse.

"That's lousy logic of binary opposition! Your question reminds me of the question of going out or going in with each foot straddling each side of a threshold[77]," he retorted.

"I just want to find out what is right and what is wrong beyond logic," I replied.

"Is it because standards are relative?" he said.

"No. Just because of the limitation of language," I answered.

"Then I will tell you again. Ascetic practice is definitely

self-abuse in every way. Self-abuse means abandoning yourself. Laozi once said, "He who devotes himself to the Tao seeks from day to day to diminish his doing. He diminishes it and again diminishes it, till he arrives at doing nothing on purpose. Having arrived at this point of non-action, there is nothing which he does not do."[78] As far as I understand it, the Way can be attained when you have nothing left to lose after repeated trials to diminish yourself."

"I think true ascetic practice should be self-centered," I said.

"Please, do not make a judgment as if you're objective. Say directly what you think.

"Sunim, let me ask you a simple question. When you follow your practice, are you aware of "diminishing"?

"Yes, I am. I think it and I feel it as well. And I try to come up with ways and means to do my practices more strictly. Like today when I decided to go on a fasting prayer retreat. Whenever I eat raw grain for my meal, I suffer intensely."

"Sunim, your "ascetic practice" is not ascetic practice at all. Laozi didn't actually practice asceticism. He just made smart analogies about it. Your ascetic practice is simply a meaningless effort mistakenly dedicated to the Way of Laozi who didn't even experience or feel it. If you're aware of or sense that you're engaged in some difficult practice, then, you've already lost it. Ascetic practice in a true sense refers to the practice that you do without the awareness that you're doing it at all."

"Well, is ascetic practice possible if you take good care of your body?" he questioned.

"There's an old saying "nothing is more important than your body, live first and then you can do everything." This may sound very materialistic and egoistic. If you look into it very carefully, though, you'll see that it expresses the universal truth of all beings very well. "I" can be found when I realize that I'm merely one of the countless beings appearing and disappearing through the endless functioning of infinite space, eternal time and inexhaustible energy. While searching for "I," I have to take good care of myself, and to do this, I'll have to practice. When I finally find myself on the path, there is no "I" but nirvana. This being so, do you really have to make a fasting retreat in your poor health?"

"By the way, what is nirvana? What is it that attracted all of us to this distant mountain?" he asked.

"I don't know what nirvana is. One thing I know is that it cannot be expressed in words. If you talk about it, already, it is not nirvana. Speaking about nirvana can be compared to blind men talking about an elephant. All we have to do is to become enlightened. Although I use some rarified expressions such as 'nirvana' or 'the other shore', I merely use it for easier communication," I said.

"Well, I'm going do my fasting retreat anyway. I am not you," he blurted out.

"Well, if you insist⋯"

At this point, there was nothing I could do about him anymore. He was beyond my reach. You couldn't win over this stubborn Seon monk unless you were enlightened. How stupid I was to have wasted my time using foolish words to reason with him!

As it turned out, the raw-food-eating monk ended his fast after only three days and left the seonbang with his pack.

"Things could've gotten worse⋯ at least he has a bit of conscience," the dwitbang josil spat out behind his back.

75   한단지보 (邯鄲之步) An episode from "The Flood of Autumn"
in *Zhuangzi*
"…And have you not heard of the young learners of Shou-
ling, and how they did in Han-dan? Before they had acquired
what they might have done in that capital, they had forgotten
what they had learned to do in their old city, and were marched
back to it on their hands and knees…" Translation from http://
chinese.dsturgeon.net

76   서시빈목(西施嚬目) An episode from "The Revolution of
Heaven" in *Zhuangzi*
"…when Xi Shi was troubled in mind, she would knit her brows
and frown on all in her neighborhood. An ugly woman of the
neighborhood, seeing and admiring her beauty, went home, and
also laying her hands on her heart proceeded to stare and frown on
all around her. When the rich people of the village saw her, they
shut fast their doors and would not go out; when the poor people
saw her, they took their wives and children and ran away from her.
The woman knew how to admire the frowning beauty, but she did
not know how it was that she, though frowning, was beautiful."
Translation from http://chinese.dsturgeon.net

77   An Episode of a famous Dharma battle between the two ancient
Korean Seon Masters – Master Seosan and Master Samyeong.
Master Samyeong wanted to test the Dharma power of his teacher
Seosan. Samyeong caught a bird and held it in his hand, asking
his teacher if he should kill the bird or not. At this question,
Master Seosan went to the threshold of his room and stood with
one foot inside and one foot outside, asking Samyeong, "Am I
going in or out?" Master Samyeong immediately surrendered to
Master Seosan and became his student.

78   *Tao Te Ching*, Chapter 48. Translated by J. Legge
www.sacred-texts.com/tao/taote.htm

THE WAY TO NIRVANA

Everyone's busy packing their back sacks in the dwitbang. The winter retreat will end tomorrow. I packed, too.

Spring is just around the corner. It's a warm and sunny afternoon. I did laundry and sat in the sun with my friend, the jigaek sunim.

I was very sad knowing that we'd part soon. He's been right beside me at every sitting session and when we slept. We also spoke over several days.

Jigaek sunim said to me.

"As far as I know, humans are supposed to rely on their own efforts to perfect themselves. But the more time I spend in the seonbang, the more attracted I am to an unidentifiable other power or mysticism. Do you think this is normal?"

"That's a difficult question," "It's something that Seon monks often experience however. The Buddha taught in the *Agamas*. 'Suppose a man is shot by a poisoned arrow and falls to the ground grievously wounded. His friends call for a doctor, but he refuses to be treated until his questions are answered: Who shot the arrow? What was the design of the bow? Where was the poison derived? and more. Well, what do you think would happen? He would die before he got his answers.

"While wasting time on such impertinent issues, the man was dying. Is this world limited or unlimited? Or does God exist, or not? Even if you had the answers, the question of endless human suffering still remains. That's the critical point of Buddha's teaching. It's very existential. Sartre said that for humans, what has become a problem is their own existence. He also said, "For Others, I am a being more than is needed, and Others are beings more than I need." He concluded that original sin is that I was born in the world where Others exist. Though cold, it is a realistic expression about human existence.

"Humans should raise questions about their

own existence, and they must answer the questions for themselves. This is the starting point of both Buddhism and existentialism. One reason why modern intellectuals pay attention to Buddhism is that while existentialism destroyed and overcame delusions about the invisible world – in other words – theology, it didn't devise dependable human guidelines to replace the commandments of God that people have lived under. It asserts that humans are independent beings thrown into the world absurdly. (No matter how wise they might be, existentialists are also sentient beings. Although they were able to depict the human condition, they couldn't posit a solution and save the world.) Another reason, which is even more fundamental, is that modern mechanistic civilization threatens the foundation of human existence by standardizing and collectivizing human lives. Buddhism points out 108 defilements and teaches a way of liberation from them."

"But, sunim. Humans must live as humans. They cannot transcend or escape from the human realm, can they?"

"Absolutely correct. Human existence cannot be transcended. But humans can be perfected and their condition harmonized. Seon arose within Buddhism for the perfection of human existence. It's possible for humans to perfect themselves through Seon. Seon is not mysticism, and it's not something controlled by an absolute being, either. It's the path to perfect human beings. It's the path to nirvana."

"You're identifying human perfection with nirvana. Granted, is nirvana real? Or is it just a possibility?" the jigaek sunim inquired.

"Existentialism asserts that everything exists as reality, not as possibility. It asserts that the world is monistic, and nothing exists behind reality. It argues that it is nonsense to talk about a substance or eternal world behind phenomena. It doesn't show a way of human perfection. This is a shortcoming of existentialism.

"Nirvana in Buddhism doesn't indicate a world beyond death. Rather, it harmonizes the absurd and indiscriminate reality of 108 defilements. Nirvana refers to the wisdom that illuminates emptiness.

"Nirvana represents the world liberated from attachment to form. Nirvana is ultimate truth and being and non-being is a relative truth. If attachment to being and non-being has something to do with life and death in this phenomenal world, entering into Nirvana means eternal liberation. *Heiler*[79] said nirvana is God's world without God and God's gift without a donor. God's world without a god implies the perfected human, and the gift without a donor refers to the contents of the perfected human."

"Don't you think the perfected human is a god? Is this why so many different gods have been created and worshipped since ancient times when humans began to think?" the jigaek sunim asked.

"There are people longing for a so-called omnipotent God and waiting for the coming of the Messiah. If such a day has already been decided, then humans are mere puppets without free will. Puppets of absolute being. Slaves of God. If Heaven is like that, I'll choose Hell where I can live with free will no matter how painful it may be. If Paradise is like that, too, I will run from it and embrace the endless path of karmic suffering."

"You're very human-oriented," the jigaek sunim remarked.

"It's because I'm a Buddhist! Buddhism starts with the human (sentient being) and ends with the human (enlightened person). Buddhism teaches the path of great liberation from the 108 defilements."

"I think I should work harder on my hwadu," said jijaek sunim.

"Absolutely. We don't really know what's going to happen even a moment from now. If this is true, how can you leave your hwadu even for a moment? If you neglect your hwadu, you are a mere sentient being. As long as you hold it, you're on the path."

We heard the sound of a *moktak*[80] announcing the dinner offering. We stood up and began to walk slowly. Though we walk slowly, we live with great urgency within.

79   Friedrich Heiler (1892-1967) A German theologian and historian of religion

80   Wooden percussion instrument shaped like a fish. Moktaks are used for rituals and signals in Korean temples.

PARTING WAYS

The winter retreat ends today. It is two a.m. Everyone's excited and rose early. The jijeon sunim is performing the *Doryangseok*[81]. His voice is crisp and clear and so is his echo. The huge Shilla bell booms. Its resonance is fathomless and its reverberations are fathomless as well.

The josil sunim began his Dharma talk after breakfast to mark the last day of the retreat. The josil sunim looked compassionate as always sitting on his Dharma Platform Seat with the Dharma staff in hand.

"One is many, many are one. Form is emptiness, and emptiness, form. These words directly express the Middle Path in Buddhism. The Middle Path is dialectical synthesis as well as harmonization of values. It's a higher and greater value beyond self and other. Here is the truth of the Mahayana. When facing opposites, the Middle Path doesn' t lead to conflict and separation; a greater value is created by the two opposites . The Middle Path is not "average" or "neutral." Its goal is to acclaim the truth, "many are one" out of the infinite teachings of Buddhism. One is many."

To sum up his Dharma talk, the Middle Path of Buddhism accords with the Great Ultimate[82] of the *Book of Changes*[83] or Zisi's[84] Mean or Aristotle's Golden Mean. Transcending opposites is one of its most important tasks. The purification of individuals and the purification of the world can only be realized this way. But it's totally up to every individual. The welfare of society cannot be attained without the purification of the minds of individuals within it.

After early lunch, the monks packed their robes and bowl into their barangs. Each departing monk was given a thousand *won* as a "traveling stipend."

It's inevitable that those who meet must part. Parting, though, promises meeting again in the future. Seon monks are likely to meet again at another seonbang as long as they remain Seon monks. I put my barang on my back, too. I climbed up here when the trail was covered with golden leaves. I'm hiking down with the jigaek sunim in the snow. As if they had to hurry a long way, most monks passed us quickly though they didn't have anyone to welcome them where they were going.

"Sunim, where are you heading?" the jigaek sunim inquired.

"I'm going to Mt. Sorak. I'm going to live in a hermitage. I want to be free of boredom and laziness. I'm going somewhere that looks like a place to be lazy but I really want to escape laziness by living there. I'm going to live a very boring, regimented life so I can liberate myself from boredom. I believe I'll have a greater chance of Enlightenment in a hermitage by myself than living with others."

"And where are you going?" I asked the jigaek sunim.

"I'm going south. I'll go to another seonbang. Whenever I become lazy, I need formal discipline, and whenever I get bored, I need the dwitbang. Whenever I dropped in the dwitbang, I couldn't help but return to practice quickly"

We parted at the foot of the steps at Woljeongsa, bowing to each other with palms together sharing our mutual aspiration for Buddhahood.

Seong-bul ha-ship-shi-o!

"May you attain Enlightenment."

Seong-bul ha-ship-shi-o!

"May you attain Enlightenment."

The south-bound monk walked into Woljeongsa. I continued on toward Gangneung, Woljeongsa behind me.

81   도량석 (道場釋) An early morning ritual in Korean Buddhist monasteries designed to awaken the world and purify the temple. A monk walks around the temple, chanting sutras and hitting a moktak. This ceremony is usually conducted at three a.m.

82   태극(太極)

83   역경(易經) or *I-Ching*

84   子思, 481–402 BCE, was a Chinese philosopher. Zisi, who was the only grandson of Confucius and wrote the *Doctrine of the Mean*.

Korean Terms
–